PAW PATROL™: PUPS SAVE A GIANT PLANT
A CENTUM BOOK 9781912707409
Published in Great Britain by Centum Books Ltd
First published 2018
This edition published 2021
3 5 7 9 10 8 6 4 2

Centum Books Ltd, 20 Devon Square, Newton Abbot, Devon TQ12 2HR, UK
9/10 Fenian St, Dublin 2, D02 RX24, Ireland
books@centumbooksltd.co.uk
CENTUM BOOKS Limited Reg. No. 07641486

A CIP catalogue record for this book is
available from the British Library

Printed in Great Britain

PUPS SAVE A GIANT PLANT

STARRING...

SKYE

RUBBLE

MAYOR GOODWAY

AND

CHICKALETTA

TRACKER

CHASE

MARSHALL

CARLOS

The PAW Patrol are travelling in the PAW Patroller on their way to see Carlos in the jungle. This is the first time that Mayor Goodway and Chickaletta have ever been to the jungle. They are very excited.

The Mayor has brought a special plant that she calls Buddy to give to Carlos as a present.

The Mayor and Chickaletta grew it themselves from a seedling. "Even your plant looks excited, Mayor Goodway," says Chase.

When they arrive at the jungle,
Carlos gives them a warm welcome.

"On behalf of
Adventure Bay, I present
you with Buddy," says
Mayor Goodway.
"What a nice gift,"
says Carlos.

Carlos tells the Mayor that plants grow very well in the jungle because there is rich soil and lots of sun and rain. It's Rubble's job to dig a hole for the new plant.

"Rubble on the double!" says Rubble and he sets to work.

The plant seems very happy to be in the jungle. In fact, it seems to have grown a little bit already!

Just then, Tracker hears animals moving in the undergrowth.

"Sounds like ... baby snakes!" says Tracker, listening hard.

The Mayor jumps in fright. She would rather stay with Buddy than go looking for snakes. Marshall doesn't look too happy about the snakes either!

"I'll just stay here and keep the Mayor company," he says. Ryder and the other pups run off to watch the snakes.

The moment they are out of sight,
the plant has a huge growth spurt.
The Mayor and Chickaletta are lifted
high off the ground on one of the leaves.

"Buddy, put us down!" shrieks the Mayor,
but he doesn't. They're stuck high up on the plant.

"I'm coming, Mayor," says Marshall. He runs as fast as he can towards Buddy and tries to climb the thick stem.

But the stem is hard to climb. Marshall slides back down to the ground again. "Maybe not," says Marshall.

Not far away, Ryder, Carlos and the pups are enjoying watching some baby snakes hatch. Ryder gets a call from the Mayor.

"What's up, Mayor Goodway?" he asks.
"Me!" says the Mayor. She explains about Buddy growing and lifting her and Chickaletta off the ground.

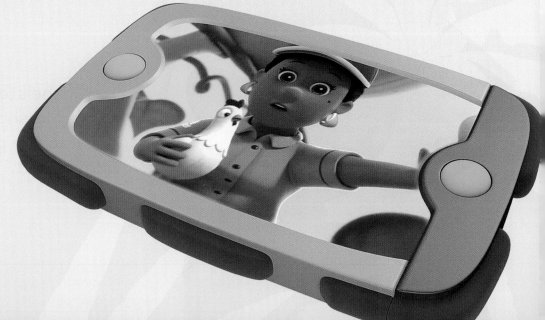

"No plant is too big, no Pup is too small," replies Ryder. "PAW Patrol to the PAW Patroller!"

"Ryder needs us,"

bark the pups, and they're off. The pups run as fast as they can back to the PAW Patroller.

Halfway up the plant, Marshall's Pup Tag flashes. He slides round and round, down the twisting stem.

He flies through the air and lands in the PAW Patroller with a crash and a giggle!

In the PAW Patroller, Ryder
explains the problem to the pups.
"For this mission, I'll need Marshall," he says.

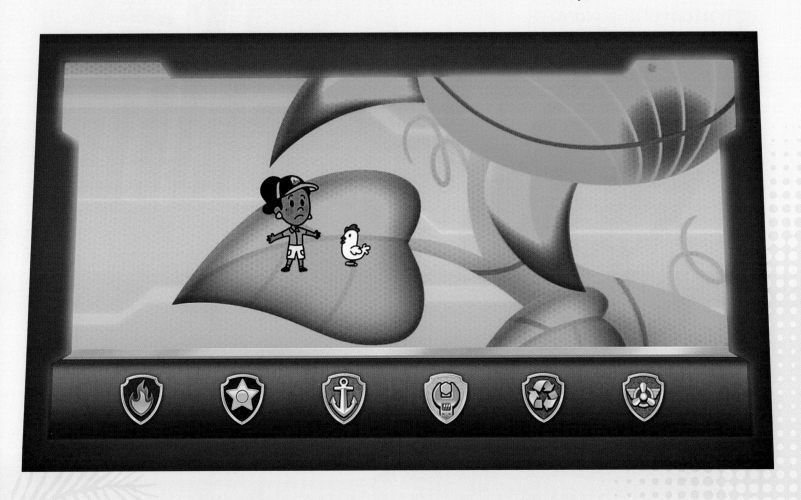

Marshall's tall fire ladder will be just what they
need to rescue the Mayor. Ryder also wants
Chase to set up his net on the ground, just in case
the Mayor or Chickaletta falls.

It's not long before Ryder,
Chase and Marshall are
ready for action at the
bottom of the plant.

"Hang on, Mayor Goodway,"
shouts Ryder. "We'll get you down."
"Net," barks Marshall. His safety net
shoots out of his cannon and into place.

"Ladder," says Marshall. His long ladder extends right up and rests on Mayor Goodway's leaf.

The Mayor is scared to climb down. Just as she gathers the courage to try she sees that a vine has grown around her feet.

Tracker uses his cables to climb up the plant
and his pliers to cut away the vines.
   The Mayor is soon free. As she starts to climb
down, the plant lurches towards her, opens
what looks like a huge, green mouth and ...

... poor Chickaletta
disappears inside!

"Buddy, how could you?" says Mayor Goodway.
"After all the water and sunshine I gave you."
But as she shouts, she loses her balance and falls
off the leaf, landing with a bounce in the safety net.

Carlos has been busy studying a book. He has worked out what kind of plant Buddy is.

"It's a Bugumlovus," explains Carlos. "These plants love to eat insects that are only found on the other side of the swamp."

That gives Ryder an idea. He calls through to Zuma.

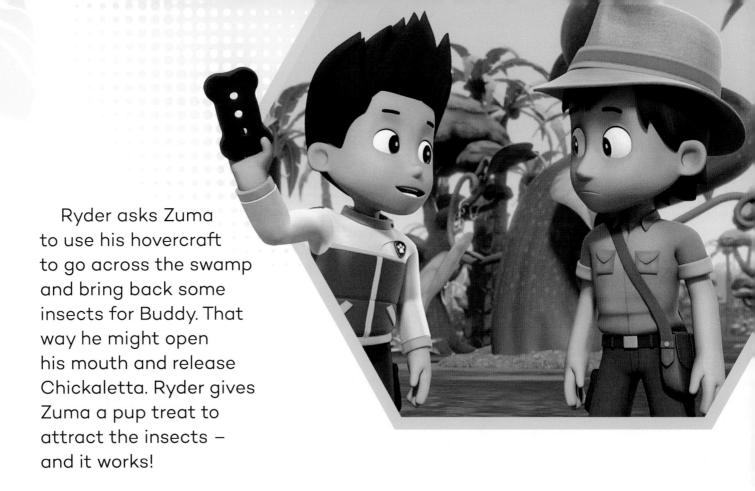

Ryder asks Zuma to use his hovercraft to go across the swamp and bring back some insects for Buddy. That way he might open his mouth and release Chickaletta. Ryder gives Zuma a pup treat to attract the insects – and it works!

As Buddy opens his mouth to eat the insects, Chickaletta flies free!

"Oh, my brave little chicken," says the Mayor. Now something needs to be done about Buddy. The soil where he is planted is too fertile, which is why he keeps growing.

"Time to go for a ride," says Rubble. He uses his rig to dig up Buddy's roots. Then Buddy is lifted out of the ground and onto the roof of the PAW Patroller.

Ryder's plan is to take Buddy to his new home on the other side of the swamp.

"Thank you for saving me, PAW Patrol,"
says the Mayor, "and for moving Buddy."

Buddy certainly looks happy
in his new home with the smaller,
insect-eating plants!
    "Whenever you have a plant
problem, just yelp for help!"
Ryder laughs.

THE END